The HOUSE that Jack Built

A Mother Goose Rhyme
Illustrated by J. P. Miller

🐦 A GOLDEN BOOK • NEW YORK

Library of Congress Control Number: 2004117867
ISBN: 978-0-375-83530-8
www.goldenbooks.com
www.randomhouse.com/kids
Educators and librarians, for a variety of teaching tools, visit us at
www.randomhouse.com/teachers
Printed in the United States of America
10 9 8 7 6 5 4 3
First Random House Edition 2008

This is the house that Jack built.

This is the cat
That chased the rat
That ate the malt
That lay in the house
that Jack built.

This is the dog
That worried the cat
That chased the rat
That ate the malt
That lay in the house
    that Jack built.

This is the cow
   with the crumpled horn,

That tossed the dog

That worried the cat
That chased the rat
That ate the malt
That lay in the house
that Jack built.

This is the maiden
    all forlorn,
That milked the cow
    with the crumpled horn,
That tossed the dog
That worried the cat
That chased the rat
That ate the malt
That lay in the house
    that Jack built.

This is the man
   all tattered and torn,
That kissed the maiden
   all forlorn,
That milked the cow
   with the crumpled horn,
That tossed the dog
That worried the cat
That chased the rat
That ate the malt
That lay in the house
   that Jack built.

This is the priest
    all shaven and shorn,
That married the man
    all tattered and torn,
That kissed the maiden
    all forlorn,
That milked the cow
    with the crumpled horn,
That tossed the dog
That worried the cat
That chased the rat
That ate the malt
That lay in the house
    that Jack built.

This is the cock
that crowed
in the morn,

That waked the priest
    all shaven and shorn,
That married the man
    all tattered and torn,
That kissed the maiden
    all forlorn,
That milked the cow
    with the crumpled horn,
That tossed the dog
That worried the cat
That chased the rat
That ate the malt
That lay in the house
    that Jack built.

This is the farmer
sowing the corn,
That kept the cock
that crowed
in the morn,

That waked the priest
all shaven and shorn,

That married the man
all tattered and torn,
That kissed the maiden
all forlorn,

That milked the cow
  with the crumpled horn,

That tossed the dog

That worried the cat

That chased the rat

That ate the malt

That lay in the house that Jack built.